P9-BVC-206

FLUFFY

written & illustrated by
Danielle Johnson

LANDMARK EDITIONS, INC.

P.O. Box 270169 • 1402 Kansas Avenue • Kansas City, Missouri 64127
(816) 241-4919

Dedicated to:
My family for all their love and encouragement;
and to my cat, Mopsy, who used to be with
our family and who gave me the idea for
the story of Fluffy.

With special thanks to Beth Finn,
my Reading Teacher at Hale Cook Elementary School,
for all her help and support to me
while I was creating my book.

COPYRIGHT © 1999 BY DANIELLE JOHNSON

International Standard Book Number: 0-933849-74-5 (LIB.BDG.)

Library of Congress Cataloging-in-Publication Data
Johnson, Danielle 1990-
    Fluffy / written and illustrated by Danielle Johnson.
    p.   cm.
    Summary: Sam loses his cat Fluffy, who is old and blind, and fears
that he will never see her again.
ISBN 0-933849-74-5 (lib.bdg. : alk. paper)
[1. Cats—Fiction.   2. Lost and found possessions—Fiction.
 3. Blind—Fiction.   4. Physically handicapped—Fiction.]

I. Title.
PZ7.J63163113F1   1999
[E]—dc21
                                        99-19124
                                        CIP

All rights reserved. Except for use in a review, neither all nor part of this
publication may be reproduced, stored in a retrieval system, or transmitted
in any form or by any means, electronic, mechanical photocopying,
duplicating, recording or otherwise, without prior written permission of
the publishers.

Creative Coordinator: David Melton
Editorial Coordinator: Nancy R. Thatch
Computer Graphics Coordinator: Brian Hubbard

Printed in the United States of America

Landmark Editions, Inc.
P.O. Box 270169
1402 Kansas Avenue
Kansas City, Missouri 64127
(816) 241-4919

Visit our Website — www.LandmarkEditions.com

The 1998 Panel of Judges

Richard F. Abrahamson, Ph.D.
    Director of Graduate Programs in
    Literature for Children and Adolescents
    University of Houston, TX

Kaye Anderson, Ph.D.
    Associate Professor, Teacher Education
    California State University at Long Beach

Barbara Diment, Library Media Specialist
    Portland Jewish Academy, Portland, OR

Jane Y. Ferguson, Editor
    CURRICULUM ADMINISTRATOR

Dorothy Francis, Instructor
    Institute of Children's Literature
    Author — METAL DETECTING FOR TREASURE

Patricia B. Henry, Teacher
    Wyoming State Reading Council Coordinator

Brian Hubbard, Associate Editor
    Landmark Editions, Inc.

Joyce E. Juntune, Lecturer
    Department of Education, Psychology
    Texas A & M University

Beverly Kelley, Library Media Specialist
    Linden West Elementary School, North Kansas City, MO

Lucinda Kennaley, Home Educator
    Kansas City, MO

Jean Kern, Library Media Specialist
    Educational Consultant, Landmark Editions, Inc.

Joyce Leibold, Teacher
    Educational Consultant, Landmark Editions, Inc.

Eathel McNabb, Teacher
    Educational Consultant, Landmark Editions, Inc.

Teresa M. Melton, Associate Editor
    and Contest Director, Landmark Editions, Inc.

John Micklos, Jr., Editor
    READING TODAY
    International Reading Association

Helen Redmond, Teacher of the Gifted
    Indian Woods Middle School, Overland Park, KS

Shirley Ross, Librarian, President Emeritus
    Missouri Association of School Librarians

Philip Sadler, Professor Emeritus, Children's Literature
    Director, Annual Children's Literature Festival
    Central Missouri State University

Cathy R. Salter, Writer and Educational Consultant
    The National Geographic Society

N.A Stonecipher, School Counselor & Psychologist
    T.J. Melton Elementary School, Grove, OK

Bonnie L. Swade, Teacher of English & Speech, Grade 9
    Pioneer Trail Junior High School, Olathe, KS

Nan Thatch, Editorial Coordinator
    Landmark Editions, Inc.

Barbara Upson, Youth Services Specialist
    Corinth Library, Prairie Village, KS

Kate Waters, Senior Editor
    Scholastic Hardcover Books
    Author — ON THE MAYFLOWER

Teresa L. Weaver, Library Media Specialist
    League City Intermediate School, League City, TX

Authors:

Carol S. Adler — MORE THAN A HORSE
Sandy Asher — WHERE DO YOU GET YOUR IDEAS?
Dana Brookins — ALONE IN WOLF HOLLOW
Clyde Robert Bulla — THE CHALK BOX KID
Scott Corbett — THE LEMONADE TRICK
Julia Cunningham — DORP DEAD
David Harrison — THE PURCHASE OF SMALL SECRETS
Carol Kendall — THE GAMMAGE CUP
Colleen O'Shaughnesy McKenna — GOOD GRIEF...THIRD GRADE!
Barbara Robinson — THE WORST BEST SCHOOL YEAR EVER
Ivy Ruckman — IN CARE OF CASSIE TUCKER
Theodore Taylor — THE HOSTAGE
Elvira Woodruff — THE ORPHAN OF ELLIS ISLAND

Authors and Illustrators:

Drew Carson — SUMMER DISCOVERY
Elizabeth Haidle — ELMER THE GRUMP
Laura Hughes — BRIGHT EYES AND THE BUFFALO HUNT
Amy Jones — ABRACADABRA
Jonathan Kahn — PATULOUS, THE PRAIRIE RATTLESNAKE
Benjamin Kendall — ALIEN INVASIONS
Gillian McHale — DON'T BUG ME!
David Melton — WRITTEN & ILLUSTRATED BY...
Jayna Miller — TOO MUCH TRICK OR TREAT
Kristin Pedersen — THE SHADOW SHOP
Lauren Peters — PROBLEMS AT THE NORTH POLE
Justin Rigamonti — THE PIGS WENT MARCHING OUT!
Anna Riphahn — THE TIMEKEEPER
Steven Shepard — FOGBOUND
Erica Sherman — THE MISTS OF EDEN —
                NATURE'S LAST PARADISE

FLUFFY

WINNER

GOLD
AWARD

1998

This is an adorable book!

I'm surprised that I like it so much because I am not inclined to care very much for "adorable books."

This book is also about a cat, and I have to admit that I am not a full-fledged cat fancier. Oh, I like cats all right, but I don't fall down and worship the ground they walk on, you know what I mean.

At home I am surrounded by "cat people" who enjoy pampering and petting their precious, purring pets. They also shower them with baby talk and cooing sounds. I don't do any of that. I suspect that is why, in my family, I am known as the "Cat Scrooge." You understand, I'm not mean to cats, and I'm not rude to them. If a cat comes over and sits next to me, I will pet it and be nice to it. I just don't want it to climb on my shoulders, or lick my hands, or put its nose against my face.

At the office I am surrounded by more "cat people." Even our judges at Landmark are among the afflicted. They always make a big fuss over the books we receive that are about cats. And, of course, when they saw FLUFFY, they adored the book! "Even the name is *adorable*!" one of them said. As one of the preliminary judges, I had no choice but to read FLUFFY. And do you know what? Surprise! I really liked the story! And I liked the illustrations, too!

As adorable books go, this one is not overly saccharine. Together, the text and the paintings tell a straightforward story about a boy and his cat. The cat is named Fluffy. She is blind, and she gets lost. The boy looks and looks for Fluffy, until finally...well...I'm not supposed to tell the ending, but I can assure you, it is a happy one.

The author/illustrator of FLUFFY is Danielle Johnson. She is adorable, too! In fact, she may be even more adorable than her book. Danielle happens to live in Kansas City. As she was adding the finishing touches to her illustrations for the publication of her book, her father sometimes brought her to our offices to work on them. She had her own private office, complete with her own personal name plaque on the door.

At first, Danielle seemed to be shy. She was always quiet and didn't talk to me very much. Then, one day her father had to leave for a couple of hours, and he left Danielle with us so she could work in her private office.

All of our authors and illustrators love the idea of having a private office, but most never stay there very long. I like to think it's because they like me, but one of my staff members bluntly said, "They probably just get lonely."

Anyway, after a while, Danielle came to my office and asked if she could paint her pictures at one of my big tables. When I said she could, she brought her paints and paper, and she sat down and started to work.

As Danielle was painting, she opened up and started talking to me. For the next hour, she talked nonstop. She told me about the plots of the scariest movies she had ever seen, which were many, and she described the most bloodcurdling scenes in vivid detail.

When I didn't pass out or throw up on the floor, I think she decided that I was "okay," and we became friends. Before she left that day, she said I could call her "Dani." Her father told me that was a high compliment, because she allowed only family members and her best friends to call her that.

One of my favorite authors and illustrators is Dani Johnson. She is my friend. I think her book is adorable! I now invite you to read FLUFFY and adore it, too.

> — David Melton
> Creative Coordinator
> Landmark Editions, Inc.

There once was a boy named Sam.
Sam had a cat named Fluffy.
Sam loved his cat.

Fluffy was an old cat, but she was still beautiful.
She had soft, orange fur.
And she had long, black whiskers.

Fluffy liked to play outside with Sam and his friends.
She was a very good cat.
She never hissed at people or scratched them.

Fluffy enjoyed playing inside the house, too.
She liked to roll back and forth on the floor.
And she really loved to chase her toy mouse.

Most cats do not like to take baths.
They don't like to be in water. But not Fluffy.
She loved to have Sam give her a bath.

Some cats scratch the furniture.
But not Fluffy.
She never scratched the chairs or the couch.

As Fluffy got older, she did not play as much.
    She liked to sleep on the windowsill. And she liked to
lie next to Sam when he was reading a book.
    Every time Sam would pet Fluffy, she would purr.

One day Sam noticed something strange.

When Fluffy walked across the kitchen floor, she bumped into the wastepaper basket.

Later that day, she bumped into one of the chairs.

Sam and his mother took Fluffy to the veterinarian.
The veterinarian examined the cat's eyes.
He told Sam and his mother that Fluffy was blind.
That made Sam and his mother very sad.

Fluffy did not seem to mind being blind.
She always acted like she was happy. But now she walked more slowly. Sam was careful not to leave big things on the floor for Fluffy to bump into.

One weekend Sam's Uncle Russ came to visit.
Uncle Russ was a nice man.
But he did not like cats.

Somehow Fluffy knew that Uncle Russ did not like her.
She did something she had never done to anyone else.
She hissed at Uncle Russ!

That night everyone went to bed early, except Uncle Russ.
He walked into the kitchen to get a glass of water.
He did not notice that Fluffy was in front of him.

And he stepped on her tail!

Fluffy hissed loudly! Then she jumped up, and she scratched Uncle Russ on his leg!

When Sam woke up the next morning, he could not
find Fluffy. He walked from room to room.
"Here, Fluffy," he called. "Here, kitty, kitty."
"Has anyone seen Fluffy?" asked Sam.

18

"She scratched me last night," said Uncle Russ, "and I threw her outside."

"Oh, no!" cried Sam. "Fluffy is blind! She might get caught by a big dog! Or she could get hit by a car!"

Everyone hurried outside to look for Fluffy. Even Uncle Russ looked for her. He was very sorry he had put her out. He did not know she was blind.

They all called, "Here, Fluffy! Here, kitty, kitty!"

But they could not find her.

That afternoon, while his father drove the car, Sam called out the window, "Here, Fluffy! Here, kitty, kitty!"

But they could not see Fluffy anywhere.

The next day Sam went outside. He called and he
called for Fluffy. But she did not come.

Sam looked for Fluffy the day after that, and the day
after that, too.

But he still could not find her.

As he walked to school each morning, he looked for her.

When he walked home from school every afternoon, he looked for her again.

The last thing Sam did each night was open the back door and call for Fluffy one more time.

Sometimes Sam would wake up in the middle of the
night. He would think he had heard Fluffy meowing.
But every time he looked outside, she was not there.

24

"I don't think we will find Fluffy," his father finally said.
When Sam thought he would never see Fluffy again, he
felt very sad. And he cried.

One winter day, Sam walked home in the snow.
When he got close to his house, he suddenly stopped.
He saw something orange on the front porch.
"Fluffy!" he called out, and he ran to the porch.

When the cat heard Sam, she meowed weakly.

She was so thin and dirty that Sam was not sure it was
Fluffy. But he picked her up anyway.

And he carried her into the warm house.

Sam set a bowl of cat food on the kitchen floor.
The cat was so hungry, she gobbled down the food!
When Sam bathed the cat, he knew it was Fluffy. She
liked the water, and Fluffy always loved to be bathed.

28

That evening Sam sat down and read a book.
Fluffy snuggled up beside him.
Every time Sam petted her, she purred.
Fluffy was so happy to be home.

Dav Pilkey
age 19

Lauren Peters
age 7

Benjamin Kendall
age 7

Amy Hagstrom
age 9

Michael Cain
age 11

Leslie A. MacKeen
age 9

Shintaro Maeda
age 8

A. Chandrasekhar
age 9

Dennis Vollmer
age 6

Alise Leggat
age 8

Walking is Wild Weird and Wacky! written and illustrated by Karen Kerber

by Karen Kerber, age 12
St. Louis, Missouri
ISBN 0-933849-29-X   Full Color

THE DRAGON OF ORD written and illustrated by DAVID McADOO

by David McAdoo, age 14
Springfield, Missouri
ISBN 0-933849-23-0   Inside Duotone

Strong and Free written and illustrated by Amy Hagstrom

by Amy Hagstrom, age 9
Portola, California
ISBN 0-933849-15-X   Full Color

ME AND MY VEGGIES written and illustrated by ISAAC WHITLATCH

by Isaac Whitlatch, age 11
Casper, Wyoming
ISBN 0-933849-16-8   Full Color

WHO CAN FIX IT? written & illustrated by Leslie Ann MacKeen

by Leslie Ann MacKeen, age 9
Winston-Salem, North Carolina
ISBN 0-933849-19-2   Full Color

ELMER the GRUMP written & illustrated by ELIZABETH HAIDLE

by Elizabeth Haidle, age 13
Beaverton, Oregon
ISBN 0-933849-20-6   Full Color

Taddy McFinley and the Great Grey Grimly written & illustrated by Heidi Salter

by Heidi Salter, age 19
Berkeley, California
ISBN 0-933849-21-4   Full Color

Problems at the North Pole written & illustrated by Lauren Peters

by Lauren Peters, age 7
Kansas City, Missouri
ISBN 0-933849-25-7   Full Color

OLIVER and the OIL SPILL written and illustrated by ARUNA CHANDRASEKHAR

by Aruna Chandrasekhar, age 9
Houston, Texas
ISBN 0-933849-33-8   Full Color

Life in the ghetto written and illustrated by ANIKA D. THOMAS

by Anika Thomas, age 13
Pittsburgh, Pennsylvania
ISBN 0-933849-34-6   Inside Two Colors

A STONE PROMISE BY CARA REICHEL

by Cara Reichel, age 15
Rome, Georgia
ISBN 0-933849-35-4   Inside Two Colors

PATULOU, THE PRAIRIE RATTLESNAKE written and illustrated by JONATHAN KAHN

by Jonathan Kahn, age 9
Richmond Heights, Ohio
ISBN 0-933849-36-2   Full Color

ALIEN INVASIONS written and illustrated by BENJAMIN KENDALL

by Benjamin Kendall, age 7
State College, Pennsylvania
ISBN 0-933849-42-7   Full Color

FOGBOUND written and illustrated by STEVEN SHEPARD

by Steven Shepard, age 13
Great Falls, Virginia
ISBN 0-933849-43-5   Full Color

CHANGES written and illustrated by TRAVIS WILLIAMS

by Travis Williams, age 16
Sardis, B.C., Canada
ISBN 0-933849-44-3   Inside Two Colors

A SPECIAL DAY written & illustrated by DUBRAVKA KOLANOVIĆ

by Dubravka Kolanović, age
Savannah, Georgia
ISBN 0-933849-45-1   Full Color

THE NATIONAL WRITTEN & ILLUSTRATED BY...AWARD WINNERS

WORLD WAR WON
by Dav Pilkey, age 19
Cleveland, Ohio
ISBN 0-933849-22-2   Full Color

JOSHUA DISOBEYS
written and Illustrated by Dennis Vollmer
by Dennis Vollmer, age 6
Grove, Oklahoma
ISBN 0-933849-12-5   Full Color

THE HALF & HALF DOG
written and illustrated by LISA GROSS
by Lisa Gross, age 12
Santa Fe, New Mexico
ISBN 0-933849-13-3   Full Color

WHO OWNS THE SUN?
—written & illustrated by— STACY CHBOSKY
by Stacy Chbosky, age 14
Pittsburgh, Pennsylvania
ISBN 0-933849-14-1   Full Color

the Legend of SIR MIGUEL
written and illustrated by MICHAEL CAIN
by Michael Cain, age 11
Annapolis, Maryland
ISBN 0-933849-26-5   Full Color

WE ARE A THUNDERSTORM
written and photographed by amity gaige
by Amity Gaige, age 16
Reading, Pennsylvania
ISBN 0-933849-27-3   Full Color

BROKEN ARROW BOY
WRITTEN AND ILLUSTRATED BY ADAM MOORE and his friends
by Adam Moore, age 9
Broken Arrow, Oklahoma
ISBN 0-933849-24-9   Inside Duotone

GET THAT GOAT!
WRITTEN AND ILLUSTRATED BY MICHAEL AUSHENKER
by Michael Aushenker, age 19
Ithaca, New York
ISBN 0-933849-28-1   Full Color

TOO MUCH TRICK OR TREAT
WRITTEN AND ILLUSTRATED BY JAYNA MILLER
by Jayna Miller, age 19
Zanesville, Ohio
ISBN 0-933849-37-0   Full Color

PUNT, PASS & POINT!
written & illustrated by BONNIE-ALISE LEGGAT
by Bonnie-Alise Leggat, age 8
Culpepper, Virginia
ISBN 0-933849-39-7   Full Color

NINA'S MAGIC
written and illustrated by Lisa Kirsten Butenhoff
by Lisa Kirsten Butenhoff, age 13
Woodbury, Minnesota
ISBN 0-933849-40-0   Full Color

JAMBI AND THE LIONS
WRITTEN AND ILLUSTRATED BY JENNIFER BRADY
by Jennifer Brady, age 17
Columbia, Missouri
ISBN 0-933849-41-9   Full Color

Abracadabra
Written & Illustrated by Amy Jones
by Amy Jones, age 17
Shirley, Arkansas
ISBN 0-933849-46-X   Full Color

THOMAS RACCOON'S FANTASTIC AIRSHOW
written & illustrated by SHINTARO MAEDA
by Shintaro Maeda, age 8
Wichita, Kansas
ISBN 0-933849-51-6   Full Color

THE SUNFLOWER
MILES MacGREGOR
by Miles MacGregor, age 12
Phoenix, Arizona
ISBN 0-933849-52-4   Full Color

THE SHADOW SHOP
written and illustrated by Kristin Pedersen
by Kristin Pedersen, age 18
Etobicoke, Ont., Canada
ISBN 0-933849-53-2   Full Color

Travis Williams age 16

Anika D. Thomas age 13

Isaac Whitlatch age 11

Elizabeth Haidle age 13

Miles MacGregor age 12

Jayna Miller age 19

Jonathan Kahn age 9

Stacy Chbosky age 14

David McAdoo age 12

Amity Gaige age 16

Bright Eyes and the Buffalo Hunt
Written and Illustrated by Laura Hughes
by Laura Hughes, age 8
Woonsocket, Rhode Island
ISBN 0-933849-57-5   Full Color

CRITTER CRACKERS
THE ABC BOOK OF LIMERICKS
written and illustrated by KATHRYN BARRON
by Kathryn Barron, age 13
Emo, Ont., Canada
ISBN 0-933849-58-3   Full Color

Glory Trail
Written and Illustrated by Taramesha Maniatty
by Taramesha Maniatty, age 15
Morrisville, Vermont
ISBN 0-933849-59-1   Full Color

CIRCUS ADVENTURES
written and illustrated by LINDSEY WOLFER
by Lindsay Wolter, age 9
Cheshire, Connecticut
ISBN 0-933849-61-3   Full Color

THE TIMEKEEPER
Written & Illustrated by ANNA RIPHAHN
by Anna Riphahn, age 13
Topeka, Kansas
ISBN 0-933849-62-1   Full Color

DARIUS The Lonely Gargoyle
written and illustrated by MICHA ESTLACK
by Micha Estlack, age 17
Yukon, Oklahoma
ISBN 0-933849-63-X   Full Color

MOUSE SURPRISE
Written and illustrated by Alexandra Whitney
by Alexandra Whitney, age 8
Eugene, Oregon
ISBN 0-933849-64-8   Full Color

DON'T BUG ME!
written and illustrated by Gillian McHale
by Gillian McHale, age 10
Doylestown, Pennsylvania
ISBN 0-933849-65-6   Full Color

The Incredible JELLY BEAN DAY
Written and Illustrated by TAYLOR MAW
by Taylor Maw, age 17
Visalia, California
ISBN 0-933849-66-4   Full Color

SUMMER DISCOVERY
WRITTEN AND ILLUSTRATED BY DREW CARSON
by Drew Carson, age 8
Roseburg, Oregon
ISBN 0-933849-68-0   Full Color

The Mists of Eden
NATURE'S LAST PARADISE
Written and Illustrated by Erica Sherman
by Erica Sherman, age 12
Westerville, Ohio
ISBN 0-933849-69-9   Full Color

THE PIGS WENT MARCHING OUT!
written & illustrated by Justin Rigamonti
by Justin Rigamonti, age 17
Hillsboro, Oregon
ISBN 0-933849-70-2   Full Color

Written & Illustrated by...
a revolutionary two-brain approach for teaching students how to write and illustrate amazing books

David Melton
96 Pages • Illustrated • Softcover
ISBN 0-933849-00-1

Written & Illustrated by... by David Melton

This highly acclaimed teacher's manual offers classroom-proven, step-by-step instructions in all aspects of teaching students how to write, illustrate, assemble and bind original books. Loaded with information and positive approaches that really work. Contains lesson plans, more than 200 illustrations, and suggested adaptations for use at all grade levels – K through college.

The results are dazzling!
– Children's Book Review Service, Inc.

...an exceptional book!
Just browsing through it stimulates excitement for writing.
– Joyce E. Juntune, Executive Director American Creativity Association

A "how-to" book that really works!
– Judy O'Brien, Teach

WRITTEN & ILLUSTRATED BY... provide current of enthusiasm, positive think and faith in the creative spirit of childre David Melton has the heart of a teacher.
– THE READING TEACH

Steven Shepard
age 13

Karen Kerber
age 12

Kristin Pedersen
age 18

Lisa Butenhoff
age 13

Heidi Salter

Lisa Gross
age 12

Duba Kolanović
age 18

Amy Jones
age 17

Adam Moore
age 9

Cara Reichel
age 15